Text copyright © 2017 by Cary Fagan
Illustrations copyright © 2017 by Banafsheh Erfanian
Published in Canada and the USA in 2017
by Groundwood Books

Groundwood Books / House of Anansi Press
groundwoodbooks.com

We acknowledge for their financial support of our
publishing program the Canada Council for the Arts, the
Ontario Arts Council and the Government of Canada.

Canada Council   Conseil des Arts
for the Arts   du Canada

ONTARIO ARTS COUNCIL
CONSEIL DES ARTS DE L'ONTARIO
an Ontario government agency
un organisme du gouvernement de l'Ontario

With the participation of the Government of Canada
Avec la participation du gouvernement du Canada | Canadä

Library and Archives Canada Cataloguing in Publication
Fagan, Cary, author
A cage went in search of a bird / Cary Fagan ; illustrated
by Banafsheh Erfanian.
Issued in print and electronic formats.
ISBN 978-1-55498-861-7 (hardback). —
ISBN 978-1-55498-862-4 (pdf)
I. Erfanian, Banafsheh, illustrator II. Title.
PS8561.A375C34 2017   jC813'.54   C2016-905745-3
C2016-905746-1

The illustrations were done in acrylic and oil pastel.
Design by Michael Solomon
Printed and bound in Malaysia

MIX
Paper from
responsible sources
FSC® C012700

A Cage Went in Search of a Bird

Cary Fagan

PICTURES BY Banafsheh Erfanian

 GROUNDWOOD BOOKS   HOUSE OF ANANSI PRESS   TORONTO   BERKELEY

For a very long time, a cage stood in the corner of an attic. It was surrounded by other discarded things — old suitcases, books, a guitar, a lamp.

And how did the cage feel? It felt useless and unwanted.

"What good is an empty cage?" it thought. "I have to do something."

The cage rocked its way over to the window. With great effort, it got up onto the ledge.

"Don't do it!" cried the suitcase.

"It's a long way down!" twanged the guitar.

"I can stay here no longer," said the cage. "Why, I was made to keep a bird, and to hang up in a nice house, and to bring pleasure. Goodbye, my friends!"

The cage jumped.

Thump!
The cage landed on the ground.
It smelled the fresh air.
It felt the warm sun.
And then the cage saw a bird.

"Dear bird," said the cage. "Wouldn't you like to come inside? I have a lovely perch for you to sit on."

But the bird just opened its beak to scold the cage.

"Why do I need your perch when I can sit on any branch in any tree I like?"

And the bird flew away.

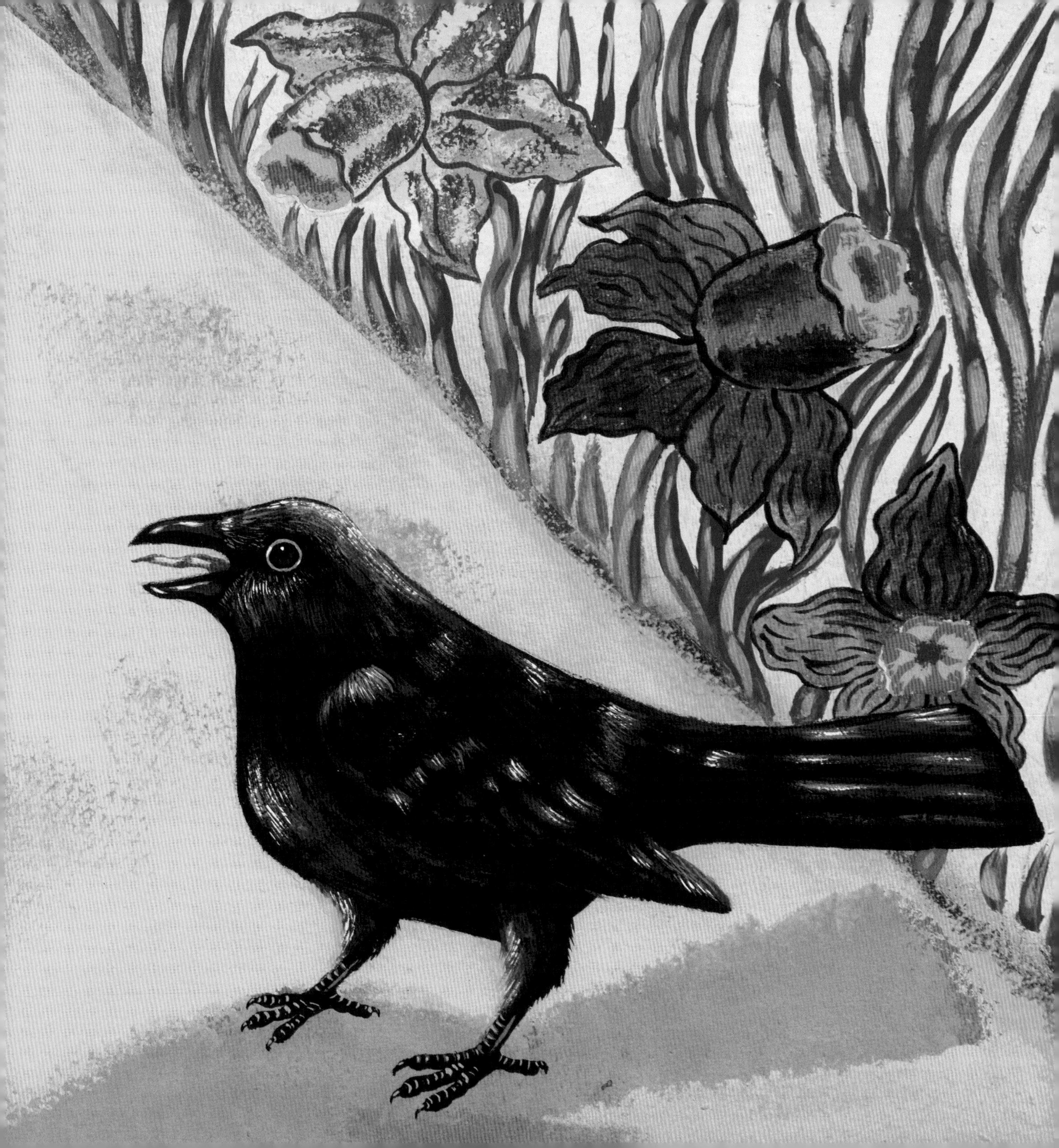

With a mighty heave, the cage rolled itself up a hill.

A bird flew past, snatched an insect from the air and landed nearby.

To get the bird's attention, the cage banged its door open and shut.

"Dear bird, wouldn't you like to come inside? In here you'll find all the food you want."

The bird tilted its head back to swallow the insect.

"There's plenty to eat around here," said the bird. "And when there isn't, I just fly somewhere else — like this!"

The bird flapped its wings and was gone.

"There is no point in staying up here," thought the cage. It began to roll down the hill, which was much easier than going up. It went faster and faster and became quite afraid. At last it crashed against a bush.

Three small birds fluttered up into the air and then settled down again. They began to peep and whistle and trill.

"Dear birds," said the cage. "Wouldn't you like to come inside? In here you can peep and whistle and trill to your heart's content."

"But we can do that now!" the three small birds said with a laugh.

They darted away, chasing one another through the air.

All was quiet.

The cage sighed. "I was empty before and I'm empty now. And what good is an empty cage?"

And then the cage felt a sort of rattling. A bird had landed right on top of it!

"Dear bird," said the cage. "If you think it's nice up there, just imagine how fine it is inside. How would you like to make me your home?"

But either the bird didn't hear, or else it was very rude, for it merely took off again.

The cage felt a patter of drops. Rain! And what if it began to rust?

It felt something again. Could it be? Yes, a bird had landed right on one of its fancy curls, of which it was so proud.

"Dear bird," said the cage. "You'll catch a terrible cold in this rain! Why don't you come inside? Cages are always kept where it's warm and dry."

"Oh, but it's dry in my nest," said the bird. "And my dear babies are waiting for me."

"Ah, that's a different matter," said the cage. "Be off to your babies, then."

The rain stopped. The cage shook
itself dry.

The night began to grow dark.

"Hoo, hoo!"

What was that? The cage looked up
and saw an owl sitting on a lamppost.

"Dear owl," said the cage. "How would you like to give up your wanderings and live inside me? We could keep each other company and become great friends."

The owl turned its head to see the cage. "I would barely fit inside you," the owl said. "I wouldn't even be able to spread my wings."

And with that, the owl lifted into the darkness.

The night grew even darker. The first star appeared, and then other stars.

The cage felt lonely.

"I wonder what the old suitcases and the guitar and the lamp are doing? At least they have one another for company."

The cage shivered in the cold.

In the darkness a bird flew by.
It landed on the ground.

The cage felt too discouraged to say a
word. But then the bird began to peep
rather miserably.

"Dear bird," said the cage. "Whatever is
the matter?"

"What's the matter?" repeated the bird. "I used to have a nice home, with food and drink and a perch to swing on. Every day I sang for my master's pleasure."

"But why are you here?" asked the cage.

"My master didn't want me anymore and turned me loose. Now I have no home. I dash from here to there, afraid of every noise and shadow. No doubt I'll soon be eaten by a cat, or die of hunger."

The bird stayed near the cage until the sun came up.

"Dear bird," said the cage, gently swinging open its door. "Do not worry anymore. Hop inside where it is warm and safe. For I have come to save you. And you have come to save me."

So the bird did.

For Sophie Fagan, free spirit. — CF

To my dearest dad, Ahmad, who means everything to me and has always been there for me. Thank you for being such a great support, Dad! Your love goes beyond words. — BE

Suggested by an aphorism by Franz Kafka:
"A cage went in search of a bird."